W9-BMK-681

A IS FOR ARK

NOAH'S JOURNEY

WRITTEN BY

Colleen & Michael Glenn Monroe

ILLUSTRATED BY

Michael Glenn Monroe

E is for Elliott.

Happy reading!

Storytime Press

Michael Monroe

Text Copyright © 2004 Colleen Elizabeth Monroe
Illustrations Copyright © 2004 Michael Glenn Monroe

All rights reserved. No part of this book may be reproduced in any manner
without the express written consent of the publisher, except in the case of brief
excerpts in critical reviews and articles. All inquiries should be addressed to:

Storytime Press
427 W. Main St.
Brighton, MI 48116
www.michaelglennmonroe.com

Book design by Graphikitchen, LLC

Printed and bound in the USA

10 9 8 7 6 5 4 3 2

Library of Congress Cataloging-in-Publication Data

Monroe, Colleen.
   A is for ark : Noah's journey / written by Colleen
Monroe and Michael Glenn Monroe ; illustrated by Michael
Glenn Monroe.
   p. cm.
   SUMMARY: Rhyming story about Noah and his adventure
building the ark and filling it with animals before the
great flood.
   ISBN 0-9754942-0-1
   LCCN 2004093738

   1. Noah--(Biblical figure)--Juvenile fiction.
[1. Noah--(Biblical figure)--Fiction. 3. Stories in rhyme.]
I. Monroe, Michael Glenn, ill. II. Title.

PZ8.3.M758Ais 2004   [E]
                 QBI04-700241

We would like to thank everyone who has helped us complete our own journey. From our parents and siblings who have given us endless support, to our three children for their wonderfully imaginative ideas. A special thank-you to Carl Sams and Jean Stoick for their advice and encouragement in getting our ship to sea.

Colleen & Michael Monroe

Writer's Note Magazine
BEST
Children's Book

A long time ago in a land far away,
a man named Noah heard from God one day.

God said to Noah, "Build a boat big and strong,
make it 75 feet wide and 6 times as long."

"Fill the boat with animals of every shape and size,
bring them on the boat two by two and side by side."

To be sure that nothing would be missed,
Noah made a special list.

He listed things from A to Z,
of everything he'd take to sea.

A is for Ark, the first thing on the list, built big and strong like God had wished.

B is for Beavers, Bears and Bats,

C is for Crocodiles, Camels and Cats.

D is for Dog, man's best friend,

E is for Elephant, with a big rear end.

F is for Family, his three sons and his wife,
the most important things in Noah's good life.

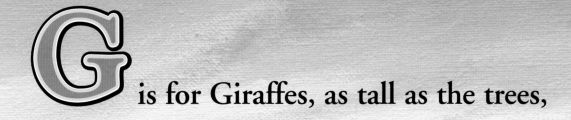 **G** is for Giraffes, as tall as the trees,

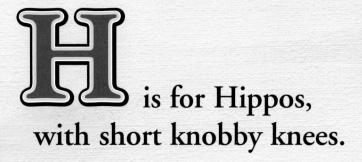 **H** is for Hippos,
with short knobby knees.

I is for Insects of every shape and size,

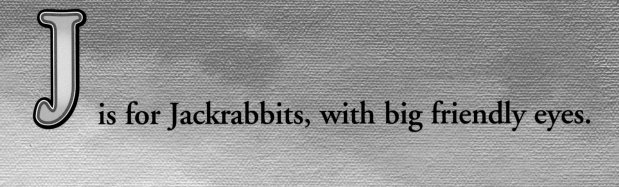

J is for Jackrabbits, with big friendly eyes.

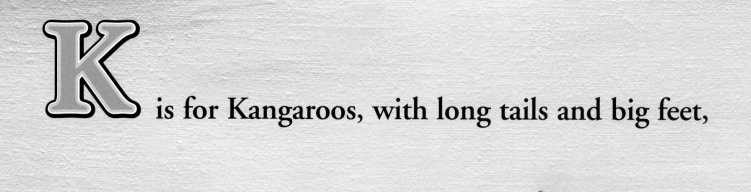

K is for Kangaroos, with long tails and big feet,

L is for Lions, with many sharp teeth.

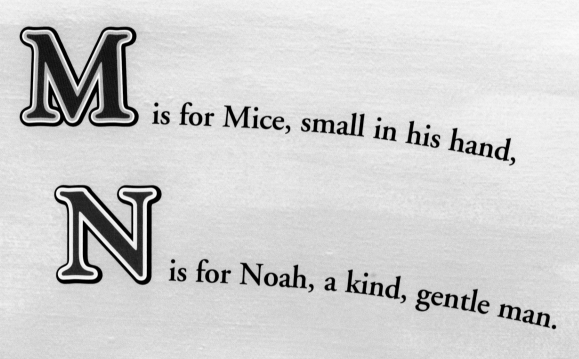

M is for Mice, small in his hand,

N is for Noah, a kind, gentle man.

O is for Ostriches, with necks thin and long,

P is for Porcupines, with quills sharp and strong.

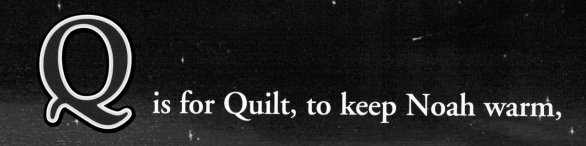

Q is for Quilt, to keep Noah warm,

R is for Rhino, showing off his big horn.

S is for Skunks, who can't help their strong smells,

T is for Turtles, safe in their shells.

U is for Umbrella, to keep Noah dry,

V is for Vultures,
   looking down from up high.

W is for Walrus,
with tusks long and white,

X on the map shows the way that is right.

Y is for Yak, with long stringy hair,

Z is for Zebra, the very last pair.

Now Noah's list is finally done.
He's filled the boat with everyone.

For forty days and forty nights,
rain covered all the land in sight.

It was almost a year that they sailed the sea,
wondering what their fate would be.

Noah sent a dove into the air,
to see if land was anywhere.

The dove returned with a branch he had found,
which showed them all there was dry ground.

The Ark came to rest upon the sand,
and two by two they touched the land.

Happy to be done with their wondrous trip,
they said goodbye to their faithful ship.

Off they went to start life anew,
and soon would be many where
once there were few.

Michael Glenn Monroe has known since a very young age that he wanted to be an artist. His realistic wildlife paintings have garnered him many honors throughout the years including Michigan Wildlife Artist of the Year, Michigan Habitat Featured Artist and Minnesota Whitetail Association Artist of the Year. His work was featured on the DNR Endangered Species print, chosen as the Michigan Duck Stamp winner, the Ducks Unlimited Stamp & Print winner and received numerous Best of Show awards. Michael's paintings have also graced the covers of over 200 magazines and been featured on dozens of television programs.

Michael's colorful illustrations have filled the pages of over 20 children's books. His first book was the popular *M is for Mitten; A Michigan ABC Book,* which was chosen by Governor Granholm for her inaugural gift.

In 2007, Michael was personally chosen by the President and Mrs. Bush to create a series of fifteen paintings to be featured in the White House Holiday Program. The original paintings were hung in the White House for the Christmas Celebration, and are now part of the permanent White House gallery. Michael was called upon again by the White House to hand-paint 1,000 Christmas ornaments for the President and Mrs. Bush to be used as personal gifts to friends and dignitaries.

Colleen Monroe credits her three children as the inspiration behind her books, especially *The Christmas Humbugs.* She is also the author of *The Wonders of Nature Sketchbook, Mr. Rabbit's Wish* and *A Wish to be a Christmas Tree,* which was read on the *Today Show* by Katie Couric and by Mitch Albom for an animated television special.

Colleen is a graduate of the University of Michigan, and spent many years in advertising before joining her husband in his art business.

A is for Ark, Noah's Journey is just one of many childrens' books the couple has worked on together.

ALSO BY

Colleen Monroe & Michael Glenn Monroe

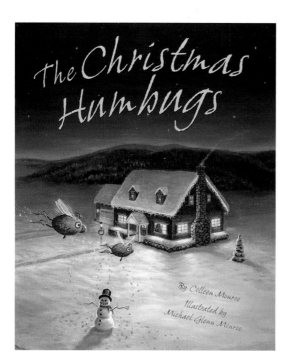

The Christmas Humbugs
U.S. $17.95 • CAN. $21.95

A Wish to be a Christmas Tree
U.S. $16.95 • CAN. $19.95

Mr. Rabbit's Wish
U.S. $16.95 • CAN. $19.95

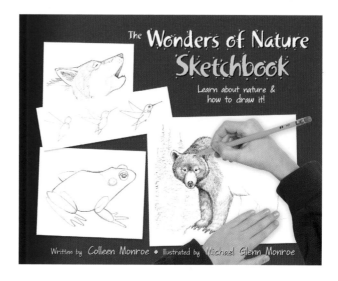

The Wonders of Nature Sketchbook
U.S. $15.00 • CAN. $19.00

Storytime Press, Inc • 427 W. Main • Brighton, MI 48116 • 810.229.1915
www.michaelglennmonroe.com